Peacock
and Crane

retold by Jay Parker
illustrated by Jane Wallace-Mitchell

Harcourt
SCHOOL PUBLISHERS

Printed in Mexico

ISBN 10: 0-15-351416-7
ISBN 13: 978-0-15-351416-6

Ordering Options
ISBN 10: 0-15-351212-1 (Grade 2 Advanced Collection)
ISBN 13: 978-0-15-351212-4 (Grade 2 Advanced Collection)
ISBN 10: 0-15-358051-8 (package of 5)
ISBN 13: 978-0-15-358051-2 (package of 5)

1 2 3 4 5 6 7 8 9 10   050   15 14 13 12 11 10 09 08 07 06

Long ago, Peacock believed he was very special because of his bright feathers with their wonderful patterns.

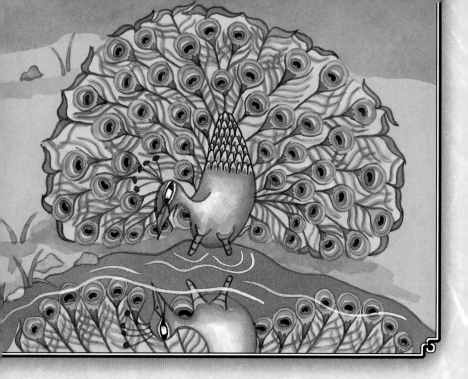

Peacock would stare at his
reflection in a puddle.

"It is clear that no other bird
is even half as beautiful as me!" he
would say. "I am the most beautiful
bird in the whole world!"

He thought that the feathers
of other birds were very dull.

Peacock was so full of himself that all day he strutted about showing off his tail. He wanted everyone to notice how special he was. He never realized that there were special things to notice in others.

One day, Crane came by. Crane had gray, ordinary feathers with no wonderful patterns or colors. Peacock felt sorry for him.

"It must be difficult for you to accept that your feathers are so dull," said Peacock. "Could you perhaps do something to brighten yourself up?"

Crane didn't mind Peacock's question though it was rather rude.

"I'm happy the way I am," Crane replied.

"Really?" said vain Peacock in surprise.

"I know you are rather beautiful," Crane said to Peacock, "but you can't fly like me."

"That's not fair!" said Peacock. "I can fly." Up he flew, rather clumsily, onto the branch of a nearby tree.

Crane flew up to join him.

"You can fly a little," agreed
Crane, "but I can fly much better
than that."

"I can fly so high and far that you might think I was a distant gray cloud in the sky. I can fly for miles, over rivers and mountains. You see, your bright feathers are not as useful to you as my dull feathers are to me."

   Peacock flew back to the ground
and spread his grand tail again.
However, he found himself suddenly
wishing that he could fly as well
as Crane.

Peacock watched Crane fly away and saw how his gray wings lifted him up easily.

Before he disappeared, Crane called out, "Some have one thing, some have another. We are all special in different ways."

For the first time, Peacock realized that what Crane had said was absolutely true.

Think Critically

1. How were Peacock and Crane alike? How were they different?

2. What words would you use to tell about Crane?

3. What did Peacock do that showed he thought he was beautiful?

4. What made Peacock change during the story?

5. Did your feelings about Peacock change during the story? How?

 Language Arts

Write a Letter Write a letter from Peacock to Crane that Peacock may have written at the end of the story.

 **School-Home Connection** Read *Peacock and Crane* to a family member. Talk about why each person in your family is special.

Word Count: 353